ALTADENA LIBRARY DISTRICT

3 9270 00190 9278

\$15.95

New 2000

DATE DUE

MAR 2 7 2000	
MAY 2 2000	
JUL 1 8 2000	
NOV 1 3 2000	
DEC 2 1 2000	
JUL 2 1 2001	
MAY 2 9 2002	
JAN - 2 2003	
DEC 1 8 2007	
FEB - 9 2008	
NOV 2 8 2009	
OCT 3 0 2012	

BRODART, CO.   Cat. No. 23-221-003

D1165266

MAR 0 1 2000

j398.2
RAT

THE WOMAN IN THE MOON

A Story from Hawai'i

Retold by **Jama Kim Rattigan**   Pictures by **Carla Golembe**

Little, Brown and Company
Boston   New York   Toronto   London

For Lenny, with special thanks for your constant support and encouragement;
and to all the children of Hawai'i, especially Kristin Wee and Jessica Sano

My thanks to Ann Rider for all her help and guidance, and to Ruth Turner,
Interlibrary Loans, Fairfax County Public Libraries, for her research assistance
— J. K. R.

For Midge Merlin, Marjie Sokoll, and Joyce Zakim in celebration of friendship

Mahalo *to: the Hambidge Center; the island and people of Kaua'i; Carol Lovell,*
Director, Kaua'i Museum; Jack Smith, of Native Plant Propagators; and to my
husband and traveling companion, Joe, who helps in so many ways
— C. G.

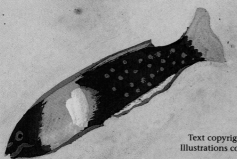

Text copyright © 1996 by Jama Kim Rattigan
Illustrations copyright © 1996 by Carla Golembe

All rights reserved. No part of this book may be reproduced in any form or
by any electronic or mechanical means, including information storage and
retrieval systems, without permission in writing from the publisher, except by
a reviewer who may quote brief passages in a review.

First Edition

Library of Congress Cataloging-in-Publication Data

Rattigan, Jama Kim.
  The woman in the moon : a story from Hawai'i / retold by Jama Kim
Rattigan ; pictures by Carla Golembe. —1st ed.
  Summary: Retells the ancient Polynesian story of how Hina, the best tapa
maker, rises above the restrictions placed on most women and goes to live in
the moon.
  ISBN 0-316-73446-2
  [1. Polynesians — Folklore. 2. Folklore — Hawaii.] I. Golembe, Carla, ill.
II. Title.
PZ8.1.R2255Wo   1996
398.2'0996 — dc20
[E]   95-21198

10 9 8 7 6 5 4 3 2 1

NIL

Published simultaneously in Canada by Little, Brown & Company (Canada) Limited

Printed in Italy

The pictures in this book were painted in gouache, an opaque water-based
paint, on Victoria cover, a 100-percent rag black paper.

Glossary

Aikanaka (AH-ee-kah-NAH-kah)
Hina's husband

Ānuenue (AH-noo-ay-noo-ay)
rainbow

auwē (AH-oo-WAY)
an expression of wonder or distress

'āwikiwiki (AH-WEE-kee-WEE-kee)
an endemic Hawaiian vine

calabash (KAL-uh-bash)
a bowl made from a gourd

Hina (HEE-nah)
a goddess

Hōkū-pa'a (HOH-KOO-PAH-ah)
the North Star

'ilima (ee-LEE-mah)
a native shrub with yellow-orange flowers

kalukalu (KAH-loo-KAH-loo)
a gauzelike cloth, considered to be of the finest
quality

kapu (kah-POO)
prohibition

kukui (koo-KOO-ee)
candlenut tree

Lauhuki (lah-oo-HOO-kee)
"rustling leaf," the mythical woman who beat
the first tapa

lehua (lay-HOO-ah)
flower of the *'ōhi'a*, a favorite native tree

mahina (mah-HEE-nah)
the moon

makahiki (mah-kah-HEE-kee)
ancient Hawaiian festival featuring athletic
contests and religious events

malo (MAH-loh)
man's loincloth

Mauna Kea (MAH-oo-nah KAY-ah)
"white mountain"; the highest peak in Hawai'i

Na Hiku (nah HEE-koo)
the Big Dipper

Na-holo-holo (nah-HOH-loh-HOH-loh)
the evening star

Na Kao (nah KAH-oh)
Orion

naupaka (nah-oo-PAH-kah)
a native mountain or seashore shrub with small
white half-flowers

'oli'oli (OH-lee-OH-lee)
much joy, happiness

'ō'ō (OH-OH)
all-but-extinct endemic honeyeaters with black-
and-yellow feathers

pā'ū (PAH-OO)
a woman's skirt or sarong

poi (POH-ee)
a staple food made by pounding taro root with
water to make a thick paste

tapa (TAH-pah)
bark cloth (modern spelling of *kapa*)

taro (TAH-roh)
plant whose bulbs are used for poi (modern
spelling of *kalo*)

uhiuhi (OO-hee-OO-hee)
an endemic Hawaiian forest tree

I luna la, i luna (EE LOO-nah lah, EE LOO-nah)
I lalo la, i lalo (EE LAH-loh lah, EE LAH-loh)
A he nani ke ao nei. (AH HAY NAH-nee kay AH-oh NAY)

Above, above
Below, below
Behold this lovely world.

On nights when the moon is round and full, some say that a man lives in the moon. But in the islands of Hawai'i, where the gentle winds tell stories from ancient times, the children know that it is not a man in the moon. A woman lives there, and her name is Hina.

"She is a beautiful goddess," the children say. "Her hair is blacker than the feathers of a mynah bird, and her eyes are shiny and brown like *kukui* nuts."

"Hina used to make the best tapa cloth in all Hawai'i," the older ones say. "It was red like fiery lava, as green as the mountains, pink like hibiscus."

"But why did she go to the moon?" the little ones ask. "And what does she do there now?"

It is true that Hina did not always live in the moon. Long ago, in the days of old Hawai'i, she made her home in a cave under Rainbow Falls. Every day Hina pounded tapa. It was hard work, but she liked turning plain tree bark into beautiful cloth. She liked decorating it with what she loved in nature, like the shapes of leaves and shells or the stripes on deep-sea fish. She often chanted while she worked, and the sound of her pounding and chanting could be heard echoing throughout the valley:

> "I luna la, i luna
> I lalo la, i lalo
> A he nani ke ao nei."
>
> (Above, above
> Below, below
> Behold this lovely world.)

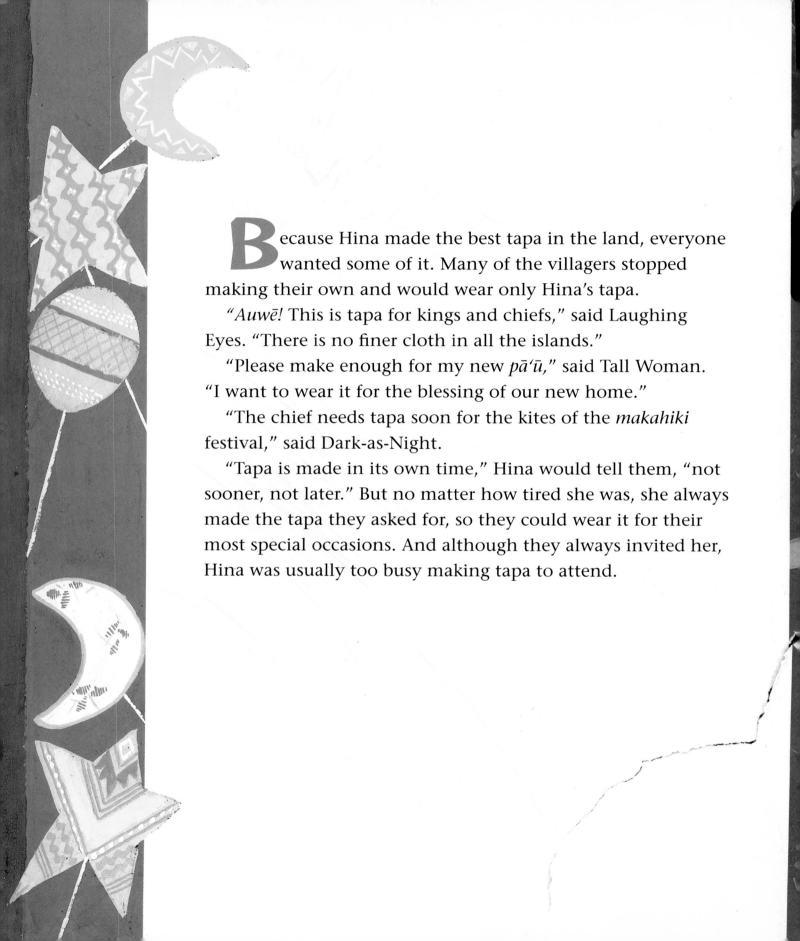

Because Hina made the best tapa in the land, everyone wanted some of it. Many of the villagers stopped making their own and would wear only Hina's tapa.

"*Auwē!* This is tapa for kings and chiefs," said Laughing Eyes. "There is no finer cloth in all the islands."

"Please make enough for my new *pā'ū,*" said Tall Woman. "I want to wear it for the blessing of our new home."

"The chief needs tapa soon for the kites of the *makahiki* festival," said Dark-as-Night.

"Tapa is made in its own time," Hina would tell them, "not sooner, not later." But no matter how tired she was, she always made the tapa they asked for, so they could wear it for their most special occasions. And although they always invited her, Hina was usually too busy making tapa to attend.

Now, most husbands in the village cooked and prepared the bark for tapa making, but Hina did not even have her husband to help her. Aikanaka-the-Wanderer was usually gone hunting or fighting in faraway places. And when he was home, he was lazy and complained about everything.

"You are slower than a trickling stream," he said, his mouth full of sweet potato. "Where is my new *malo?* And my cape? And why haven't you pounded the poi?"

As much as Hina loved making beautiful tapa, she was weary of doing Aikanaka's work and of making so much tapa for the entire village. She also did not like living in a place where so many things were *kapu,* or forbidden, for women. Because she was a woman, she was not allowed to eat fresh coconut, roast pork, or golden ripe bananas. She could not pray or eat with her husband or go with him on his adventures, like fishing for the deep-sea shark or hunting the wild forest boar.

Hina longed for a place where such wonderful things in life were not *kapu* for her. She wanted a home where she did not have to work all the time but could spend her hours enjoying the world she loved: the big bowl-shaped sky full of stars, the dancing shadows the sun made on the *uhiuhi* leaves, and the laughing ripples the dolphins made on the sea. If only she could have such a home, Hina knew she would once again enjoy making tapa — tapa with colors like the purple sea urchin and patterns like the rolling hills of the ocean.

That is why one day brave Hina decided to look for a better home than the cave under Rainbow Falls. She rose early with the morning moon, built the fire, then prayed to her guardian, Lauhuki, who beat the first tapa, hoping that somehow her tapa would tell her what to do.

Hina picked up the sheets of bleached tapa that had dried in the sun and taken in the evening dew. She loved their smooth whiteness; they were as white as the snow upon the mountains.

As she pounded the tapa, the image of Mauna Kea, the highest mountain on the island, kept appearing before her. "Perhaps this is where I am meant to live," she thought. "On top of this mountain, I could look down and watch everything I love: the deep, dark forests, the thundering waterfalls, the fishponds and taro fields."

So finally Hina put down her beater and walked many miles, following the river upstream to the foot of Mauna Kea. She found the narrow, spiraling path that led to the top.

The air grew cooler and cooler the higher she climbed. When she finally stepped onto the frozen whiteness at the peak, the cold sliced through her like a thousand ivory needles. *"Auwē,* this place is much too cold and much too white to make a good home," she thought. And so she quickly descended and returned to her cave.

By morning moon, Hina had decided that her new home must be high like the mountains, but a place of color and warmth. Again she prayed to Lauhuki, hoping her tapa would help her find the way. She picked up the delicate *kalukalu* cloth and held it up to the sunlight to study the watermark. How should she decorate it? With the dark purple from the *naupaka* berry or the bright pink from the raspberry? Decorating was what Hina loved most. Design and color made the tapa come alive.

As she dipped her bamboo stamp into her colors and pressed it onto the cloth, she waited for the image of her new home to appear to her. She dipped and pressed, dipped and pressed, but when it was time to catch shrimp for dinner and fill the water gourds before nightfall, she still did not know where her home should be. A light rain began to fall, so Hina quickly put away the *kalukalu* and hurried to the stream.

There she saw pretty ribbons of color reflected in the water. Hina looked up to see a rainbow arching high into the sky, reaching up to the sun's warmth and light. Perhaps Lauhuki had guided her there; perhaps she should go to the sun! She dropped her *'āwikiwiki* net and walked to where the ribbons rose from the grass. She took one step and found the path firm. One step, then another, higher and higher. She stepped into all the colors she loved: the red of *lehua,* the orange of *'ilima,* the bright yellow of the *'ō'ō* bird, and the green of pandanus leaves. Surely this rainbow would lead her to the place she dreamed of!

She climbed faster and faster, but as she rose, the sun's scorching rays burned her skin and the blazing heat melted all her strength. She fell onto her hands and knees and tried to crawl. But the sun was too strong. Hina slid back down to earth.

She lay on the grass until the air grew cool and the full moon awakened her. The sun, like the mountains, would not make a good home. "Lauhuki," she prayed for the third time, "please show me where to look now."

When she felt stronger, Hina returned to the cave, only to find Aikanaka angry. "I had to fill the water gourds myself!" he shouted. "Where is the shrimp?"

This time, Hina surprised her husband. She took the gourd from his hands and poured the water into her own mouth. When it was empty, she looked up at the full, round moon and saw a night rainbow forming. It was as clear as the *kalukalu* that she had started decorating. "The moon," she thought, "is high like the mountains, but full of light and color like the sun. Yet it does not burn like the sun." Now Hina was sure that Lauhuki had answered her prayers. She quickly filled her calabash with all she treasured and picked up her favorite tapa mallet and board.

"Where are you going?" asked Aikanaka. He knew by the calabash that she was going far.

"To my new home," she answered. Then she hurried to the field, with Aikanaka following.

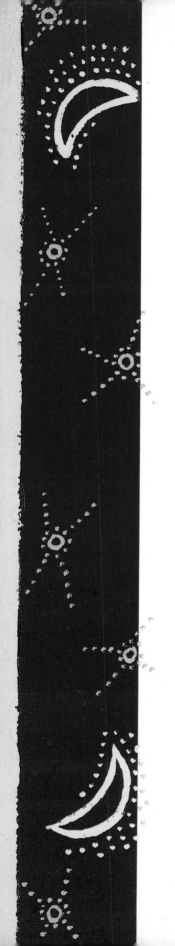

There she saw the moonbow, with all the colors she loved glittering by cool moonlight. She saw the myriad of stars, the same stars her ancestors had steered their canoes by to find new lands. Unafraid of the journey ahead, she whispered to the rainbow, "Blessed Ānuenue," and stepped up onto the misty arch. Her husband stared in disbelief.

She found the path steady and inviting, but Aikanaka, who tried to follow her, was too heavy for the trail. He jumped up and tried to grab her foot but fell back. Hina kept climbing, and as she rose higher into the evening sky, she called upon the stars: "Na Kao. Na Hiku. Hōkū-paʻa. Na-holo-holo." One by one, they showed her the way. When she stepped into the moon, her spirit was finally free. She had found her home at last.

And that is how Hina the goddess came to live in the moon, and why the Hawaiians call the moon *mahina*. She is happy in the quiet heavens, where she can see all that she loves on earth: the streams, waterfalls, and mountains; the forests, fields, and craters. From there she can watch over all the children of Hawai'i, as they learn how to put what they love most into their work, like the shapes of leaves and shells or the stripes on deep-sea fish.

You see, from that time on, the villagers had to make all their own tapa. And although no one has yet made cloth quite as beautiful as Hina's, she has become the inspiration for the artists of Hawai'i, young and old.

Now when it rains on the rooftops of Hawai'i, the children say that Hina is sprinkling her bark with much *'oli'oli*. When it thunders, they say she is rolling away the stones that keep her tapa from blowing away. And when there is lightning, they say Hina is shaking out the folds in her cloth.

And if the grown-ups don't believe them, the children of Hawai'i will point to the full moon, for there you can clearly see the beautiful goddess sitting with her board and mallet. She is busy making tapa, and the fine, fleecy clouds that drift by are really pieces of tapa Hina has set out to dry.

AUTHOR'S NOTE

The story of Hina, the Woman in the Moon, is known throughout Polynesia in a variety of versions. This retelling is based most closely on the Hilo version, from Hawai'i. Hina's story came to the islands with the earliest migrating families and was orally preserved during Hawai'i's ancient prehistory by skillfully trained storytellers.

To the basic tale I have added details of ancient Hawaiian life, with special emphasis on the making and uses of tapa. Strips of bark from the paper mulberry tree were first soaked in seawater or fresh water, then pounded with a club-shaped beater on a large flat stone. After becoming suitably softened and joined, the strips were laid out in the sun to dry. These would then be rolled up and stored until the second soaking, when the pieces were wrapped in ti leaves and soaked in fresh water until they fermented. For the second beating, a square wooden mallet with different carvings on each side was used to further refine the cloth, which could then be dyed or decorated in a number of ways.

The result was the best tapa in the Pacific and, most likely, the world. It was of the finest, most even texture and displayed the most variety in pattern, design, and color combinations. The Hawaiians also invented notable techniques for decorating tapa, such as the use of block printing with carved wooden or bamboo stamps.

Hina's ascent to the sun and the moon via the rainbow are both true to the original; for dramatic balance I added her initial ascent to the peak of the white mountain. To support my interpretation of the story, I elaborated on Hina's motivation to find a new home. Her struggle aptly illustrates the ancient Hawaiians' desire to escape the oppression of the *kapu* system by elevating tedious, menial work to high art. That she is female makes her story strikingly contemporary, providing an insightful link between past and present.

Sources

Beckwith, Martha. "Hina Myths," in *Hawaiian Mythology*. Honolulu: University of Hawaii Press, 1976.

Colum, Padraic. "Hina, the Woman in the Moon," in *Legends of Hawaii*. New Haven: Yale University Press, 1937.

Pukui, M. and Korn, A. L., eds., trans. *The Echo of Our Song: Chants & Poems of the Hawaiians*. Honolulu: University of Hawaii Press, 1973.

Thompson, Vivian L. "The Woman in the Moon," in *Hawaiian Myths of Earth, Sea, and Sky*. Honolulu: University of Hawaii Press, 1966.

Westervelt, William. *Legends of Maui, a Demi-God*. Honolulu: Hawaiian Gazette Co., 1910.